THE DARK REALM

TusK
THE MIGHTY MAMMOTH

l thanks to Allan Frewin Jones

For Rosie

www.beastquest.co.uk

ORCHARD BOOKS
338 Euston Road, London NW1 3BH
Orchard Books Australia
Level 17/207 Kent St, Sydney, NSW 2000

A Paperback Original
First published in Great Britain in 2008

Beast Quest is a registered trademark of Working Partners Limited
Series created by Working Partners Limited, London

Text © Working Partners Limited 2008
Cover illustration by Steve Sims © Orchard Books 2008
Inside illustrations by Brian@KJA-artists.com © Orchard Books 2008

A CIP catalogue record for this book is available from
the British Library.

ISBN 978 1 40830 002 2

5 7 9 10 8 6

Printed in Great Britain

The paper and board used in this paperback are natural recyclable
products made from wood grown in sustainable forests. The
manufacturing processes conform to the environmental regulations
of the country of origin.

Orchard Books is a division of Hachette Children's Books,
an Hachette UK company.

www.hachette.co.uk

Tusk
THE MIGHTY
MAMMOTH

BY ADAM BLADE

ORCHARD BOOKS

WELL

CITY
GATES

MALVEL'S
CASTLE

THE WESTERN CITY

GATEWAY TO
AVANTIA

THE RIV

MARSHES

Gorgonia

REBEL SETTLEMENT OF KALOOM

...SE ...OREST

...RAINFOREST

VALLEYS

THE BLACK OCEAN

RUINED CASTLE

Welcome. You stand on the edge of darkness, at the gates of an awful land. This place is Gorgonia, the Dark Realm, where the sky is red, the water black and Malvel rules. Tom and Elenna – your hero and his companion – must travel here to complete the next Beast Quest.

Gorgonia is home to six of the deadliest Beasts imaginable – minotaur, winged stallion, sea monster, Gorgon hound, mighty mammoth and scorpion man. Nothing can prepare Tom and Elenna for what they are about to face. Their past victories mean nothing. Only strong hearts and determination will save them now.

Dare you follow Tom's path once more? I advise you to turn back. Heroes can be stubborn and adventures may beckon, but if you decide to stay with Tom, you must be brave and fearless. Anything less will mean certain doom.

Watch where you step…

Kerlo the Gatekeeper

PROLOGUE

"Feel my blade!" Marco slashed and stabbed with his wooden sword, made from a tree branch. "There! I have defeated another enemy of the Gorgon rebels!"

His mother's voice rang out from the nearby settlement. "Marco! Get back on watch!"

With a sigh, Marco crammed his sword into his belt and climbed back up the lookout tree, an oak that stood at the edge of the forest. From its branches he could peer down on the small rebel camp where he lived and see right across the forest, all the way to the northern hills.

The rebel camp was in a heavily forested part of Gorgonia. The leaders of the rebellion came here to make plans for the overthrow of Malvel, the Dark Wizard.

Marco's job was very important. If he spotted any Gorgonian guards, his task was to run and warn the Seniors – the men and women who governed the camp. The rebels' weapons would be thrown into a pit and covered with leafy branches, while the leaders would quickly disguise themselves as ordinary hunters and traders.

Marco shifted in his perch. He pulled his tunic close about his neck to ward off the cold wind. A movement on a far hilltop caught his eye. He peered into the distance, but couldn't quite make out what it was. He climbed higher, then gave a gasp of amazement and delight.

It was a huge creature, covered with scales that shimmered. Vast leathery wings stretched wide, jet-black against the red Gorgonian sky. Puffs of white smoke came from its nostrils.

"A dragon!" Marco murmured. He had never seen a dragon before, but he loved the stories he had been told of the beautiful, legendary Beasts – and the creature that stood on the far hilltop was most definitely a dragon!

"It's amazing!" Marco said. But where had it come from? There were no dragons in Gorgonia.

He had to let the Seniors know what he had seen. He was about to clamber down the tree when he spotted a disturbance on the far edge of the forest. Trees waved and shuddered, as though something huge were pushing through them.

As he watched, a gigantic creature came stamping out of the forest. It was a mammoth as large as a moving house, its back covered in thick brown hair that hung in shaggy tangles to its feet. The mammoth lifted her head, sending her trunk writhing up into the sky as she let out a deep battle cry.

Then she thundered up the hillside towards the dragon. Marco could see scars and old wounds on the mammoth's ears – but what he especially noticed were her long, curved tusks. As she charged, they sparkled and glinted like gold.

The dragon turned, lifting its head. Then it opened its wings, preparing to take to the air. But it was too late. Her head down, the mammoth crashed into the dragon's scaly side. She jerked her head up, catching the dragon with her long tusks, heaving the startled Beast onto its side. Marco watched in dismay as the mammoth wrapped her strong trunk around the dragon's neck and dragged the helpless creature into the forest.

"Let it go!" Marco shouted.

The mammoth's head lifted sharply. Marco gave a gasp of alarm. The monster had heard him! Small, red eyes peered across the forest, filled with anger and evil. Then the Beast charged through the trees, pushing them aside as she headed straight for Marco.

The oak shook as the evil mammoth's huge head hammered into its trunk.

There was a tearing noise as the deep roots were wrenched out of the ground. The tree began to tilt at a dangerous angle. Marco lost his footing and hung on with his arms.

But the Beast had struck the tree with such force that her golden tusks had become embedded in the trunk. She twisted her head, trying to pull herself free. A thick, clear liquid was oozing from her tusks and dripping down from the tree. It gave off a terrible, toxic stench.

The tree was now at such an angle that Marco could let go and drop safely to the ground.

Picking himself up, he raced back to the village.

But as he ran, he saw something else that made his heart thud. Marching along the track was a company of Gorgonian guards...

CHAPTER ONE

TO THE RESCUE!

"Tom!" Elenna called with a smile. "If you don't stop playing with your new friend, we'll never get started on our Quest."

Tom grinned back at her. "You'd be the same if your shadow suddenly came to life!" he said, watching the fleeting black shape as it vanished around a corner of the castle.

His shadow had leapt into action

the moment Tom had fitted
Kaymon the gorgon hound's
white jewel into his magic belt.

Tom's vision blurred, then he
suddenly realised that he could see
two different viewpoints at the same
time. With his own eyes, he could see
the wall of the castle, but he could
also see through his shadow's eyes.
He was able to scan the land of
Gorgornia, stretching away behind
the castle.

"So that's my latest magic skill!"
Tom gasped. "I'll be able to send
my shadow ahead to check for
danger. Hey!" he called. "Come
back here, please!"

The shadow bounded back around
the corner and skidded to a halt at
his feet.

"You're going to make a useful

addition to the team!" Tom laughed, as his shadow reattached itself to him. He turned and walked back to where Elenna and his stallion, Storm, were waiting.

Elenna looked questioningly at him. "Do you know where our next Quest will take us?"

Before Tom could reply, the air between them began to ripple like water. Light blazed for a moment and then an image of their friend, the good wizard Aduro, appeared in front of them.

"Is Silver with you?" Elenna asked anxiously. Her wolf had been badly hurt in their last Quest, and Nanook the snow monster had taken him through the gateway into Avantia to be healed.

"He is quite safe," Aduro reassured her. "He is being well looked after. But a new evil Beast awaits you. She is a formidable foe. Her name is Tusk."

"Is she a mammoth?" Tom asked. He had seen the great shaggy animals occasionally in Avantia.

"Yes," Aduro said. "But a mammoth unlike any you have ever imagined."

"What do you mean?" asked Elenna.

The air began to ripple again, and the image of the good wizard flickered and trembled. "Alas, I must go," he called, his voice fading. "My magic is weakening. Good luck, my friends – and be careful. You are going into greater danger than you suspect."

The image disappeared.

Tom's heart sank. These brief visits from Aduro always reminded him of how far he was from home. Then he shook himself. *There's no time to waste*, he thought. A new Quest was waiting for them!

"At least I know Silver is all right," Elenna said. "Do you think the Gorgonian map will show us where we have to go?"

"I hope so," Tom said. He felt a vibration in his shield. He looked at the six tokens, given to him by the good Beasts of Avantia, that were embedded in it. The scale of Ferno the fire dragon was glowing red.

"Ferno is in danger!" Tom said. He took out the map that Malvel had given them. They were never sure if it would show them a true path or lead them into deadly peril – but it was the only guide they had.

Spreading out the map, Tom saw a small image of the fire dragon in a region of thick forest.

"That's no more than a day's ride north," Elenna said. She pointed to a red circle drawn on the map at the southern edge of the forest. "And it's close to the rebel camp that Odora marked for us."

"Yes," Tom agreed, remembering the rebel girl who had aided them in their Quest to defeat Narga the sea monster. "That's the one thing on this map we know we can trust!"

He leapt into Storm's saddle.
"Come on. We have another good
Beast to rescue!"

Elenna sprang up behind him.
With a loud neigh, Storm set off at
a gallop.

"We'll have to pass close to the
rebel camp," Elenna said. "Do you
think we should stop there for food
and water?"

"That's a good idea," Tom said.

Soon they were moving through
a land of rolling hills and forested

valleys. Tom looked at his shield. The dragon scale was glowing more darkly now. He had a sense of foreboding as Storm galloped on beneath the red Gorgonian sky. Suddenly his mind was filled with a dark vision of Ferno writhing and crying out in pain.

"Hurry, boy!" Tom urged.

"What's wrong?" Elenna asked, clinging on as the stallion went even faster.

"I don't think Ferno has long to live," Tom called over his shoulder. He couldn't keep the concern out of his voice. "I hope we get to him in time!"

Could their Quest be over before it began?

CHAPTER TWO

LIFE AND DEATH

The hills and valleys sped past,
but Tom could see from the map
that they were still some distance
from the forest where Ferno was
being held.

"Take the reins," he told Elenna,
passing them behind his back. "I'll go
on ahead. Storm will run faster
carrying just one of us."

Without waiting for Storm to stop,

Tom jumped out of the saddle. He leapt fearlessly through the air, landing lightly and rolling through the grass. In a moment he was on his feet again. The token from Arcta the mountain giant that was embedded in his shield had protected him from the fall.

The magical golden armour Tom had won on his last Quest was back in Avantia and closely guarded in King Hugo's palace. But Tom had retained the powers it bestowed upon him, and now the golden leg armour gave him the ability to race ahead of the galloping horse.

It was thrilling to be able to run so quickly, feeling the wind in his hair, sensing the trees and boulders flashing by as he sprinted over hills that jutted into the red sky like sun-bleached bones. He felt as though he could run for ever!

Soon the steep valleys between the hills became more stony, and Tom realised that the barren ground was scattered with the skeletons of rotting creatures. The air was filled with the putrid stench of stagnant water. At last he saw the great forest ahead of him. It was a dismal sight, and smelled mouldy even from a distance. Tom shivered; it was easy to imagine the hideous creatures that lurked under cover of those gloomy trees.

He looked back and was glad to see that Storm was close behind.

The three companions made their way down the hillside towards the forest.

"This place has an evil feel," Elenna murmured, peering towards the trees. "Tom, look – everything is dead!"

"Not quite everything," Tom said, shuddering as he stared at the great poisonous-looking ferns that climbed up the rotting trees, choking the life out of the blackened, shrivelled leaves.

"I recognise those plants," Elenna said, her voice trembling. "They're called snake ferns. They grow fast and strangle everything they touch."

Tom nodded. "But Ferno is here somewhere. We have to go in," he said, pushing his own fears aside. "Come on, we don't have much time."

He stepped under the heavy canopy of branches. The trees were bunched together and the gloomy forest stank of decay. The only things that moved were flabby toads that dripped slime as they hopped among the litter of dead undergrowth.

A dull vibration shook the forest, followed by a heavy boom. Tom stopped, looking at Elenna. Another boom sounded, and then another. The ground trembled and the trees shook around them.

"Footsteps," Tom said, staring into the darkness. "Tusk is near!"

Storm whinnied nervously and stepped back. Tom stroked the

frightened horse's neck. "It's all right," he murmured soothingly. "Don't be scared."

Holding the reins, he moved forwards again, Elenna close at his side with an arrow in her bow.

"Be careful not to touch the snake ferns," Elenna warned him. "They'll grab you if they get the chance, and once you're caught, there's no getting free again."

Tom nodded and drew his sword. The stink almost made him retch, and the tree trunks that pressed in around them were dripping with a thick, sticky red sap that looked like blood.

They made their way deep into the sinister forest, pushing through large rotting plants. Green light seeped weakly through the branches. Still the tremors shook the forest.

"We have to get to Ferno," Tom said. "But how will we ever find him in this dreadful place?"

"You could try calling to him," Elenna suggested.

"Good idea!" Tom declared. "Torgor's red jewel will help me understand him." He took a deep breath and placed his hand on the scarlet gem in his belt. "Ferno!" he shouted.

Suddenly his ears were filled with the groaning of the trapped dragon.

"I can hear him!" he said, his heart aching at the pitiful sound. "He's asking for help."

"Is he saying anything else?" Elenna asked.

Tom frowned, listening hard to the dragon's voice in his head. "There's something about…twin blades," he said.

"What does that mean?" Elenna wondered.

"I don't know," Tom said. "But there's no time to worry about it now." He pointed into the crowded trees. "I'm sure his voice is coming from that direction. Follow me!"

He plunged through the undergrowth, leading Storm and

using his sword to sweep aside the
huge dead plants that rotted under
the trees. He was desperate to get
to the dragon as quickly as possible.

Then a terrible scream rang out
behind him.

"Elenna!" Tom gasped, spinning
around. "No!" he shouted as he saw a
thick snake fern draw Elenna up into
the high branches, its vicious tendrils
coiled tightly around her ankles!

CHAPTER THREE

AN IMPOSSIBLE CHOICE!

Tom ran back to where Elenna was hanging. The long snake fern had reeled her right into the treetops, pulling her up far above his head. She was dangling upside down, squirming and twisting as she tried desperately to get free.

Tom came to a halt beneath her, staring up in alarm.

"Don't worry!" he called up. "I'll
get you down! Are you all right?"

"I'm not hurt," Elenna gasped, her
face red and her eyes bulging. "The
horrible thing took me by surprise,
that's all!"

A snake fern spooled down towards
Tom like a long thin tongue, its end
twitching. Tom swung his sword at
the evil plant, cutting through it.
Green sap sprayed out as the fern

pulled away from him, writhing as it retreated back into the treetops.

There was no time to lose. "Grab my hands!" Tom called as he sprang upwards, using the power of the magical golden boots to propel him through the air.

He managed to catch hold of Elenna's hands, but almost immediately, she let out a piercing yell. "It's not going to work," she cried. "The ferns are tightening around my legs! They won't let go!"

Tom hung from her grip, watching in dismay as a long tendril of snake fern came creeping down Elenna's body and coiled itself around her neck.

He swung his legs, desperately hoping that their combined weight would rip Elenna loose from the ferns.

"Tom, don't!" Elenna choked as the

fern gripped harder around her neck. "It's strangling me! Let go, please!"

Reluctantly, Tom released Elenna's hands and dropped down to the ground. Elenna brought her hands up to her throat and forced her fingers under the tightening fern, pulling at it and gasping for breath.

Tom stared up at her. What could he do now? Even with the power of the magic boots, he couldn't leap high enough to cut through the ferns that were holding her.

The heavy footsteps were still booming through the forest, making the ground shake. And Ferno's voice was still calling weakly in Tom's head. He had to think quickly.

"I'll throw you my sword," Tom called up to Elenna. "Then you can cut the ferns!"

"No," gasped Elenna. "If I let go of the fern around my neck, it'll throttle me before I can cut myself free. I'm all right for the moment. Go and save Ferno!"

Tom hated the thought of leaving Elenna in such danger. If only Silver were here, he could send the loyal wolf in search of Ferno while he helped his friend.

As Tom hesitated, the dragon's voice grew louder in his mind and the booming footsteps shook the trees around him.

"The footsteps are getting closer," Elenna called down. "Tom, go and find Ferno – quickly!"

"I'll be back as soon as possible!" called Tom. "Hold on, Elenna. Come on, boy!" He leapt into Storm's saddle and urged the brave horse through the trees, towards the cries of the dragon.

Tom kept his sword ready, hacking and slashing at any ferns that came too close. The wicked plants moved away from him as he rode past, and then closed in again behind him. Tom knew that, without his sword, the ferns would have swarmed over him by now.

Finally, he saw Ferno through the trees. The great dragon was huddled against a trunk, snake ferns coiled all around his body so that he could hardly move. He looked exhausted. The evil tendrils were tearing at his scales and twisting around his limbs and wings. But at least he was alive!

Ferno lifted his head as he caught sight of Tom, and feeble puffs of grey smoke wafted from his nostrils.

"He can't breathe fire," Tom gasped.

The good Beast was helpless.

"I'll save you," he shouted, brandishing his sword. "Come on, Storm!"

The stallion neighed and plunged forwards. Soon Tom's bright blade would be hacking through those deadly plants and Ferno would be free!

But then a vast shape came smashing out of the trees to their left. At first, all Tom saw were flying branches and whole trees, uprooted and thrown through the air. Then, lunging through the chaos, came the most immense Beast Tom had ever seen.

Tusk came thundering forwards, her huge trunk lifted as she roared, her feet crushing everything in her path.

The evil Beast was heading directly towards them!

CHAPTER FOUR

BEATEN!

Tusk's broad, shaggy back was as high as the tallest trees. Her trunk rose up over the branches like a monstrous snake ready to strike. The thick grey skin of her head was laced with old battle scars, and her huge ears were torn and ragged at the edges.

When she opened her mouth to roar, the air was filled with the stench of her breath. Tom found himself staring in terror down a great red throat, wide enough to swallow him whole. But most fearsome of all were her long, curved, golden tusks, their sides scored with deep scratches, their points razor-sharp. Now he understood what Ferno had meant by twin blades. From their ends dripped thick, slimy liquid. It stank horribly!

The mighty Beast careered towards Tom, an evil glint in her eyes. He only had time to raise his shield in defence before she was upon him.

Storm reared up, neighing in fear, and lurched to one side. Tom gasped with relief as the mammoth's head just missed them, her trunk rearing up as she bellowed with rage. Then his stomach dropped as he felt himself slip from the saddle.

"No!" Tom cried. He threw out his hands to break his fall and felt the skin being scraped off his palms as he crashed through the dead plants. The force with which he landed drove all the air out of his lungs and he lay gasping on the forest floor, his ears ringing and his bones jarring. Only the power of the golden armour had protected him from serious injury!

Storm was bucking and rearing, neighing furiously and kicking out with his hooves. Tom could see Ferno struggling uselessly, held tight by the ferns. The dragon's angry voice filled his head.

Tusk ignored the horse and the dragon, turning instead to fix her red eyes on Tom. He scrambled to his feet, backing away through the trees, his shield up, his sword in his fist.

"Come on! I'm ready for you!" he shouted.

The mammoth stamped towards him, her golden tusks scything through the trees. But even as Tom struggled to think of a way to fight the Beast, he noticed an amber jewel embedded in one of the tusks. Another token for his magic belt!

But how was he going to get hold of it?

Then a familiar mocking laugh echoed through the stifling air of the forest.

"Malvel!" Tom hissed, looking around him for some sign of the Dark Wizard.

"You will never defeat Tusk," said the cruel, cold voice. "She will crush you like an insignificant insect!"

Anger flared through Tom. He brandished his sword and shouted, "While there is blood in my veins, I will defeat every Beast you send!"

Malvel's laughter filled his ears, but Tom wasn't going to turn back from his Quest.

Tusk was standing in an area of crushed trees, watching Tom with her evil eyes. Storm stood to one side, pawing the ground anxiously.

Tom sprang towards the mammoth, leaping high, his sword whirling. The power of the golden boots sent him soaring above the tusks, and he landed on the Beast's trunk.

Tusk roared in fury, but before she had the chance to shake him loose, Tom jumped again, this time landing on her head. He dropped to his knees, one hand clutching at the Beast's coarse hair to help him keep his balance. He stared in astonishment at the deep scars that cut into the monster's thick hide. How many battles had this huge creature fought and won?

I have to end this fight quickly! Tom thought. Was his sword strong enough to pierce Tusk's skull?

He lifted his blade, ready to plunge it down into the Beast's head.

But Tusk was too quick for him. Her trunk came sweeping back, as thick as a log. Tom ducked, but the trunk smashed into his shoulder and knocked him onto his back. Before

he could regain his footing, Tusk
shook her head, trying to throw
him off.

"I won't let you!" Tom cried. He
clung grimly to the Beast's ear,
desperate not to fall under those
pounding feet. He could see Ferno
letting out cries of distress and
struggling wildly in the loops of
snake fern. The good dragon was
trying to come to his aid.

Suddenly Storm ran forwards,
rearing up on his hind legs and
beating at the mammoth's sides with
his hooves. But it was hopeless –
Tusk seemed hardly to notice Storm's
blows. Then the Beast reared up on
her back legs, high above the trees,
swinging her great head in a final
effort to throw Tom loose. Her
enraged roaring shook the forest.

Tom felt his grip weakening. He scrabbled with his feet, but couldn't find a foothold. Tusk came thundering down onto all fours. The shock of the impact broke Tom's hold and he fell to the ground.

He looked up, horror-struck. The great feet of Tusk were rearing up again, and when they stamped down they would crush him to death!

CHAPTER FIVE

POISON!

At the last minute, Tom rolled aside, the blood pulsing in his temples.

"I won't give up!" he gasped.

He heard Elenna's voice calling from across the forest. "Tom! Are you all right?"

"Yes!" he shouted back.

Storm was still neighing wildly, and beating at the mighty mammoth with his hooves.

Using every muscle he had, and the power of the golden boots, Tom sprang up once more and regained his footing on the evil Beast's great head. Ferno let out a delighted roar and Tom turned to see the trapped dragon struggling even more fiercely against his bonds.

"Come on, Ferno!" Tom urged the good Beast. "You can do it!"

Tusk gave a bellow of anger. Then she turned from the dragon and went lumbering off through the trees, Tom still clinging grimly to her head.

Tom was being taken away from his Quest!

But Storm came galloping after them, foam at his lips and his eyes blazing as he chased the great mammoth through the trees.

As Tusk thundered along, Tom had to duck in order to avoid the falling branches and flying splinters of smashed trees.

He soon realised that the mammoth was approaching the place where the snake ferns held Elenna captive.

Gripping the coarse hair on the Beast's head, Tom stared ahead. Yes! He could see Elenna now. The snake ferns still held her tightly in their deadly grip.

Elenna twisted round to look at Tom. "Hold on tight!" she shouted.

Tusk came to a halt, her great feet pounding the earth as she peered through the trees. She had heard Elenna's voice. Then her trunk went up and she let out an ear-splitting bellow as her red eyes caught sight of Elenna, dangling upside down in the treetops. The mammoth moved towards her, ripping up trees with her trunk as she went.

Tom had to do something!

Getting carefully to his feet, Tom balanced himself on the great swaying head. He had one chance to save Elenna. He swung his arm back and sent his sword spinning through the air. The blade sliced through the ferns that were holding her. But it wasn't enough! One thick tendril still gripped her by the ankle.

Tom watched as his sword struck a tree and went tumbling to the ground. *I've lost my weapon, and Elenna's still not free!* he thought desperately. He snatched hold of Tusk's left ear and wrenched at it with all his might, trying to force her to turn aside. But even using every ounce of his strength, Tom had no effect on the evil Beast. Then Tusk's trunk came swinging back towards him.

It struck him a vicious blow, sweeping his legs out from under him and sending him plunging to the forest floor.

Dazed and gasping for breath, Tom saw Elenna struggling wildly. Her face was bright red from being held upside down for so long. He staggered to his feet and ran after Tusk, desperate to help his friend. Storm came racing up, and Tom leapt into the saddle, shouting at the top of his voice, "Tusk! Leave her! It's me you want!"

But the evil Beast ignored him. Tusk's long trunk reached out for Elenna, but before it was able to grab her, Elenna tore frantically through the final green tendril and plunged through the air. But as she fell, she knocked her arm against one of the mammoth's golden tusks. Its gleaming point pierced Elenna's skin and Tom saw red blood bubble up.

"No!" Tom shouted, as his friend

landed with a thump on the forest
floor and lay still. He jumped from
Storm's back and bounded forwards,
snatching up his sword from where it
had fallen. He ran in close to Tusk's
hind leg and drove the point of the
blade deep into the mammoth's foot.

Tusk let out a bellow of pain that shook the ground.

Tom wrenched the sword out and thrust it in again, seeing thick red blood spurt from the wounds.

The mammoth reared up, roaring with anger as the sword dug deep into her flesh, then pulled away, her head twisting around and her trunk crashing through the trees.

But Tom was too quick for her. He bounded away through the forest, running in a curve that took him to where Elenna had fallen.

He pulled her under the cover of some thick bushes.

"Thank you," Elenna whispered weakly.

"We're not safe yet," Tom said, looking anxiously at her. He quickly examined the wound on her arm. He

62

could see that it was infected. The liquid that dripped from the evil Beast's tusks must be poisonous!

He had to do something to help Elenna. But what?

CHAPTER SIX

ESCAPE INTO DANGER!

With a surge of hope, Tom remembered the rebel camp near the forest's edge. Surely someone there would be able to help?

But he had to act quickly. Tusk was close by, still bellowing with pain. He knew that at any moment the Beast's evil thoughts might turn towards them.

"Can you walk?" he asked Elenna.

She struggled feebly trying to stand up. "No," she groaned. "My legs have gone numb!"

"Don't worry," Tom said. "I'll carry you. We're going to the rebel camp."

"It's too far," Elenna gasped. "You'll never manage it."

A fearsome bellow blasted through the forest, and the hammering of huge feet shook the ground.

"Tusk is coming!" Tom cried. How would they get away in time?

Then the sound of hoofbeats came echoing through the trees. Tom looked up – Storm had found them!

"Good boy!" Tom called as the stallion came to a halt at their side. "Stay with Elenna. I'll see to Tusk!"

Tom ran from cover, stepping out into the path of the mammoth, his sword raised high. The evil Beast was bellowing with frustration and pain, her trunk swishing, her eyes blazing like furnaces. Blood oozed from her injured foot, leaving pools of thick gore where she trod.

Tom ran in close, striking at her poisonous tusks with his sword. The blade cut deep scores in them. Tusk raised her trunk, preparing to bring it down on him in a fatal blow.

"You'll never catch me!" Tom shouted as he dashed towards a patch of dense snake ferns. At the last moment, he leapt into the air. Tusk lumbered after him, but became entangled in the mass of fern. As she tried to pull herself clear, more and more ferns came snaking down towards her, coiling around her tusks, gripping her trunk, reaching for her head and body.

"It worked!" Tom panted as he landed safely on the forest floor. The more Tusk pulled and strained, the more tightly the ferns wrapped themselves around her.

He ran back to where Elenna and Storm were waiting. Gently lifting Elenna in his arms, he placed her on Storm's back.

"Hold on tight," Tom told her, pushing back a lock of hair from her pale face. Elenna smiled weakly and nodded. "Storm – follow me!" he ordered, turning away. *Elenna mustn't see that I'm worried about her*, he thought.

Tom ran through the trees, Storm close behind. The forest rang with the sound of Tusk's furious bellowing. Tom knew it was only a matter of time before she broke free and thundered after them.

They came out of the forest and Tom saw that the rebel camp, with its high fence of sharpened wooden stakes, was ahead of them. He brought Storm to a halt and lifted Elenna down from the saddle. Her face was grey and she was shivering.

"Elenna?" he murmured. Although her eyes were open, they were glazed and blank. The poison was working fast!

Tom took Epos's talon from his shield. It had the power to heal all wounds. He touched it to his friend's swollen arm. Elenna groaned but nothing happened.

This Gorgonian poison must be too strong, he thought. He left Elenna resting against a tree, with Storm watching over her. Then he ran towards the camp. The gates were shut and there was no sign of life.

"Hello!" he called, hammering desperately on the gates. "I need help!"

He knew he was putting the rebels in danger by shouting out like that and drawing attention to their camp, but he had no choice. He had to save Elenna!

No one answered. Was the camp deserted? Had the rebels fled?

He stared up anxiously at the tall gates. There was no way he could climb over them. How was he ever going to get into the camp?

I'll send in my shadow, thought Tom. *He'll find out what's happening in there.*

Tom felt a curious sensation in his feet as his shadow peeled itself free, scaled the fence and dropped out of sight. Soon he began to see through the shadow's eyes as it wove between the huts. Where was everyone?

Then the shadow peered out from behind a hut. Tom's breath hissed through his teeth. Now he could understand why no one had answered his calls for help.

All the rebels had been lined up in an open space in the middle of the camp. Armed Gorgonian guards were watching over them, while more guards ransacked the huts, searching for weapons.

Tom's heart quickened as he saw the tall, thin boy who was in command of the guards. It was Seth! Tom had encountered him before in his previous Quests; he was one of Malvel's most trusted followers.

At that moment one of the guards shouted and pointed. He had seen the shadow! Seth spun around, his blue eyes blazing.

"Capture it!" Seth shouted. "Don't let it escape!"

"Come back!" Tom whispered urgently. The shadow turned and ran. A few moments later, the wooden gates of the camp were flung open and a troop of guards came running out, carrying swords.

His plan had gone horribly wrong. Instead of helping Elenna, he had led them into another perilous situation. He had to get his friend to safety.

Tom turned to run back to Elenna and Storm – but found he couldn't lift his feet. No matter how hard he tried, his soles remained glued to the ground.

He realised with horror that this must be a side-effect of the magic. So long as he was separated from his shadow, he was helpless!

CHAPTER SEVEN

AN OLD ENEMY

Seth ran ahead of the guards, drawing his sword and making towards Tom with an evil smile. Tom struggled hard, but he still couldn't move.

Seth was a good swordsman. Tom knew he wouldn't survive if he was unable to move, no matter how desperately he tried to twist his body to defend himself.

But then Tom's shadow came

leaping and bounding through the grass. For a moment, Seth and the shadow were neck-and-neck, each only ten paces away from where Tom stood frozen.

"Come on!" Tom urged.

His shadow put on a final spurt, springing ahead of Seth. It gave a twisting leap into the air and landed at Tom's feet.

Tom turned on his heel and bounded to the side just in time, avoiding Seth's blade as it sliced the air at his throat. Snarling with rage, Seth lifted his sword high and brought it slashing down towards Tom's head. Instinctively, Tom lifted his shield to block the attack, then dug his heels into the ground and thrust out with his shield, throwing Seth's blade to one side. In the next moment, Tom brought his own sword up, aiming for Seth's evil heart!

But Seth was too skilled to be caught out so easily. He danced aside, knocking Tom's sword away and spinning round with his sword held out in both hands, the sharp blade slicing towards Tom's neck.

Tom ducked as the razor-edged blade bit the air above his head. He hoped that the miss would throw Seth off balance, but as Tom moved in, Seth leapt out of reach.

They glared at one another.

"I will enjoy killing you!" Seth snarled.

"I feel sorry for you if killing gives you pleasure," Tom retorted angrily. "But I will never be your victim!"

Seth lifted his sword high and charged at Tom, howling with anger and hatred.

Tom stood firm, gripping his sword and raising it as Seth brought his blade scything down. The two swords clashed, the impact numbing Tom's arms and jarring his shoulders.

They were face to face. Tom looked into Seth's furious pale eyes. The boy's mouth twisted into an ugly grimace as he used all his strength to try to force Tom's sword back.

But Tom was not afraid. Grunting with effort, he hammered his shield into Seth's body, following through with a stab to Seth's chest.

But Seth knocked the sword aside and stepped forwards, his blade swinging. Tom leapt back just in time to avoid a swipe that would have taken his head off his shoulders.

The Gorgonian guards were moving towards them, swords up and ready.

"Keep back!" Seth shouted to his men. "He's mine!"

Tom smiled grimly; at least the guards weren't about to overwhelm him. But if he defeated Seth, Tom knew that they would be ready to attack.

He glanced over his shoulder. Elenna was lying in the grass with Storm standing over her. The noble stallion was tossing his head and whinnying as he saw his master in danger. But Storm would not leave Elenna's side unless Tom called him. If only Silver were with them! He might have been able to help beat off Seth's attack.

Seth charged once more, forcing Tom back. Blow after blow clanged on his shield as he fought to hold his ground. Every thrust and lunge Tom made was fended off by Seth. How long could Tom survive?

Then Tom spotted something that lifted his spirits. The rebels were pouring from the gates, armed with bows and arrows. Seth's men had left the rebels unguarded – and now they were about to pay the price for their carelessness.

"Surrender now!" Tom snarled at Seth.

The evil boy's eyes glittered with

malice. "Never," he hissed. "Throw down your sword before I cut you up!"

There was an echoing twang as every rebel loosed his bowstring. Suddenly the red Gorgonian sky was thick with black arrows.

Seth spun round, staring in alarm at the aerial assault.

"Stop the archers!" he howled to his men. "Attack them!" But the guards were thrown into panic as the arrows rained down upon their armour.

Tom knew he had to make the most of the rebel attack. He raced to where Elenna lay helpless in the grass, lifted her limp body into the saddle and led Storm under the cover of the forest.

"We need to get away from those

guards," he muttered, as he squatted behind a thick tree trunk.

A second volley of arrows darkened the sky. The guards were racing about in terror.

Seth took a few steps towards the forest, searching for Tom among the trees. But then he looked over his shoulder – if he did not act quickly, his men would be mown down by those flying arrows!

He shouted a final curse at Tom, then ran back towards his men. "Guards of Gorgonia," he shouted. "Follow me!"

He ran away from the camp, his men following as the arrows hissed through the air around their ears.

"We will meet again!" Seth howled to Tom. "And on that day, you will die!"

There was cheering from the rebels as the Gorgonian guards fled. A few of the rebels ran out towards the scattering guards. Tom recognised one of them, a small, slender figure racing ahead of the others.

It was Odora, the rebel girl who had helped them in their fight against Narga the sea monster. She must have joined up with the other rebels at the camp. Tom left his friends to emerge from the cover of the trees and meet her.

"Elenna is hurt," Tom said, coming to a panting halt. There wasn't time to say anything else in greeting.

"What's happened to her?" Odora gasped.

At that moment the forest shook with the roaring of the enraged Beast.

"She was cut by the tusk of a huge mammoth," Tom explained. "The wound is poisoned."

"Don't worry," Odora said. "There's a medicine woman in the camp. Help me carry her there!"

"I can't come with you." Tom turned, staring through the thick trees. "I have to go back and face the evil Beast who did this, and I have to rescue another good friend!"

More of the rebels had arrived by now.

"Go," said Odora, nodding her head in understanding. "Do what you have to do. We'll take Elenna to the camp."

Tom led them to where Elenna and Storm were waiting. One of the men took Storm's reins and began leading him out of the forest, Elenna's body draped across the stallion's neck.

Tom knew he could trust Odora and the rebels. He only hoped they could help Elenna before the poison did its worst.

He watched them return to the camp. Then he turned and walked into the forest.

Did he have the strength to fight Tusk alone?

CHAPTER EIGHT

NEW ALLIES

Tom pushed his way through the trees. He could hear the roaring of the evil Beast, and feel the ground trembling from the pounding of her massive feet. Although he couldn't see her, he knew she must have broken free from the snake ferns. He pressed on, heading deeper into the forest.

Dread filled him, but he didn't

hesitate; his destiny lay ahead of him and he marched on through the trees to meet it.

After a while, a sound behind him made him freeze. He peered into the undergrowth. Someone was there!

"Show yourself!" he commanded.

Odora stepped out of the shadows. Behind her were twenty or more men and women from the rebel camp. Tom saw that some were armed with swords and bows, but others carried only simple weapons – pitchforks, axes and sticks. Many of them had long coils of rope slung over their shoulders, weighted at one end with fierce grappling hooks.

"We want to help you," Odora said. "Most of our people have stayed behind to guard the camp, but we couldn't let you fight the great mammoth alone. We want to defeat Malvel's power, too."

Tom smiled. "Thank you," he said. "Come on – as quietly as you can."

He strode ahead with Odora beside him and the others following. The roaring of the mammoth grew gradually louder and Tom could see trees thrashing about. She was close now!

As they went deeper into the forest, Tom could hear the plaintive cries of the captured dragon.

He sent his thoughts out to the good Beast. *While there is blood in my veins, I will not let you die!* He could tell that his words gave comfort to Ferno.

He waited until all the rebels were gathered around him. "We must split into two groups," he explained. "We need to strike Tusk from both sides at once. Use your ropes to try to bring her down – but make sure that you avoid her poisonous tusks!"

Tom put Odora in charge of one band of rebels, and led the other group himself. They split up and went creeping through the forest.

Finally they saw Tusk. She was roaring and stamping among the crushed trees. Torn vines trailed from her limbs and hung over her broad back. Tom could see that she was too engrossed in her battle against the snake ferns to spot the people creeping towards her.

He gestured to Odora. She waved back and a few seconds later the two groups of rebels flooded into the open space.

Tusk bellowed as she finally caught sight of her attackers, her golden tusks glinting dangerously in the sunlight.

You're too late! Tom thought, hope surging through him. "Use your ropes!" he shouted as the rebels came in close to the huge Beast.

Rope after rope went flying up, the hooks digging into the monster's flesh.

"Climb onto her back!" shouted Odora.

Rebels swung up on the ropes, attacking Tusk with swords and pitchforks.

"Use your bows!" came another shout.

Arrows were fired, but they sprang back off her thick hide. Axes pounded the Beast, but Tusk hardly seemed to feel the blows as she shook rebels off her back and

threatened to trample others
underfoot.

"She's too strong!" wailed one man.
"We'll never beat her!"

"Yes, we will!" Tom shouted. "Don't
despair!"

He moved in towards the Beast's
great head, watching those poisonous
tusks. He hoped that the attack
would confuse Tusk enough for him
to be able to get in close and deliver a

fatal thrust to the creature's throat.

But Tusk was not so easily beaten. She thrashed about, the ropes coming loose and the rebels swinging helplessly from her back.

A cold, cruel voice sounded in Tom's ears. It was Malvel, returning to taunt him. "You will never defeat me!" he cackled.

"I will always defeat you!" Tom shouted back, springing towards the Beast's head. He hacked at the mammoth's tusks, trying to get in close enough to stab her. But no matter how hard he fought, he couldn't get past the tusks and the swiping trunk. He saw the light of triumph glittering in the mammoth's red eyes.

The rebels were falling back now, their weapons useless against the mighty Beast. A blow from her trunk sent Tom sprawling, his sword slipping from his fingers. Tusk seemed as powerful as ever.

Tom struggled to his feet, his shield up to ward off another crushing blow. If only Elenna were there with him! Without his friend it was as if half his strength and determination were missing.

Another blow from the mighty trunk knocked him to his knees. The rebels were doing their best, but their weapons had no magic, and the arrows, pitchforks and sticks were bouncing uselessly off Tusk's hide.

He heard Malvel laughing at him. He had failed. All was lost!

But then, as Tusk raised a mighty foot ready to crush the life out of him, Tom saw a slender figure come riding through the trees on a stallion.

It was Elenna and Storm!

CHAPTER NINE

BATTLE TO THE DEATH!

An arrow flew from Elenna's bow. The shaft sank deep into Tusk's forefoot and the great Beast reared back, her ferocious red eyes glittering as a second arrow cut through the air, striking her other front foot.

Tusk backed away, her roars changing to bellows of agony as she tried to pull the arrows from her feet with her trunk. But it was too big to grip the arrows, and all she did was drive the shafts deeper into the tender flesh of her feet.

Tom brandished his sword. "Attack!" he called to the rebels.

Odora let out a battle cry and leapt towards the mammoth. The other rebels joined in, hurling weapons and slashing at her hide. The huge monster stumbled back through the trees, her vicious, poison-dripping tusks gleaming.

Storm cantered up to Tom. Elenna looked down at him, her eyes shining.

"You're better!" Tom said in amazement.

"The medicine woman had an antidote to the poison," she said. "I feel fine. Come on, let's finish the job!"

Tom ran alongside Storm as they joined the attack on the retreating mammoth.

The rebels were all around the Beast now, some with scarves across their faces to protect them from the horrible stench of her matted hair. They stabbed at her feet with their pitchforks and swords, driving her deeper into the forest.

Above Tusk's roars, Tom could hear Ferno's mournful voice in his head. The dragon was very weak; his struggles against the snake ferns had drained all his strength.

But as Tusk retreated, Tom realised that she was moving towards the place where Ferno lay imprisoned.

Tom leapt in close to the Beast's head, thrusting with his sword, dancing aside as the cruel tusks swept through the air and the trunk hammered into the ground. He stabbed at her feet once more, cutting bloody wounds, driving the Beast back as she tried to escape his darting blade.

In her agony, Tusk lifted herself up on her rear legs. She towered over them, filling the sky. Then she staggered, unable to keep her balance. For a terrible moment, Tom thought she was going to crash down on top of him. But one back leg buckled under her and she toppled onto her side, smashing trees to splinters and rocking the ground as she fell.

As the trees were torn down, Tom saw that Ferno was lying close by, still struggling among the ferns, his wings flapping weakly. The mammoth fought to get up, but as she did so her tusks tore through the snake ferns that held the dragon, ripping them to shreds.

"The ropes!" Tom shouted to the rebels. "Tie Tusk down while she's still on the ground!"

Ropes coiled over Tusk's high side, the grappling hooks digging in as the rebels fought to prevent the evil

Beast from getting to her feet.

Tom leapt through the air, using the magic of his golden boots once more, and landed on Tusk's neck. He caught hold of her ear and twisted her huge head so that her tusks pierced the ground.

"You will do no more harm with your poison!" Tom shouted, and jumped off her head, swinging his sword. The blade cut cleanly through one of the tusks. The mammoth's bellow was deafening, but Tom swung his sword again. As he chopped off the second tusk, the entire bulk of the Beast glowed with a blazing green light.

Tom shut his eyes as the glow exploded through the forest, and when he reopened them, the mammoth was gone. In her place

was

"It'

from S

Tom's si

the archw

hills of Ava

under a blue

A joyful roa

Ferno, rising up

snake fern, his b

magnificently, a bu

from his nostrils.

e can

. He turned and
rebels gazing
ough the arch. Tom
ad an idea. *I can help these*
e thought.

This gateway will take you to
freedom," he called. "But you must
go now – the gate will only be open
for a short time."

Odora stepped forwards. "But what
about the rest of our companions –
the other rebels?"

"There's no time to gather them,"
Tom explained. "It's now or never!"

Odora nodded. She gave Tom and
Elenna a quick hug, then beckoned to
her friends. They gazed at each other
for a moment or two, hesitating, then
followed Odora through the arch.

Tom turned to Elenna. "I could never have defeated Tusk without you!" he said.

Elenna nodded, smiling. "We're quite a team!"

But her smile faded as she looked at something over Tom's shoulder. He turned.

Kerlo the gatekeeper was standing under the trees, watching them.

"I wondered when you would come," Tom called, as the one-eyed man strode forwards with his cane in his hand.

But Kerlo's face was grim.

A cold fear filled Tom's heart – something was terribly wrong!

CHAPTER TEN

THE GATEKEEPER'S WARNING

Tom gazed uneasily at the tall gatekeeper as he leaned on his cane. The light of the emerald arch was reflected in his one good eye.

"Was that wise?" asked the old man.

"How can you ask?" Tom said. "The rebels are fighting against Malvel. They're good people – they deserve to find a better life!"

"Good people?" Kerlo rumbled. "Are you sure? What if they do not wish to be ruled by King Hugo? What will happen to Avantia then?"

Tom stared through the shimmering emerald arch, but Odora and the rebels had already moved out of sight. Surely Kerlo was mistaken. The rebels wouldn't cause problems in Avantia – would they?

Tom turned back to the gatekeeper,

but the ragged man had vanished into the shadows of the forest.

"Don't let him worry you," Elenna said. "You've done well. You've liberated Ferno and you've destroyed another of Malvel's evil Beasts. Aduro would be proud of you."

Tom nodded, but he still felt uneasy. A delighted roar from Ferno interrupted his thoughts. The dragon came towards them, his eyes bright with pleasure, his scales glossy and shining once more. He lifted his long snout and let out a burst of flame that lit up the gloomy sky. Evening was approaching, and the red Gorgonian sky was darkening rapidly. The sparkling emerald arch was glowing even more brilliantly in the gathering gloom, but Tom knew it would soon fade.

"You must go home now, Ferno!" Tom called to the dragon.

Ferno flapped his wings and gave another happy roar. Then he bowed his head in thanks to the two friends before flying through the emerald gateway. There was a final swish of his tail and then he was gone.

"Another Quest completed," said Elenna.

Tom nodded. "But I'd like to get out of this forest before night falls," he said.

Storm whinnied in agreement. None of them wanted to spend the night near the deadly snake ferns! Tom took the reins and the three companions walked through the trees, heading for the rebel camp.

A sound at their backs brought them to a halt. Tom drew his sword and Elenna put an arrow to the string of her bow. They waited in uneasy silence as something drew closer.

A grey shape sprang out of the darkness.

"Silver!" cried Elenna, dropping her bow as her beloved wolf came leaping towards them. He almost knocked her off her feet as he bounded around her, barking and wagging his tail, his eyes gleaming.

It looked as though his stay in Avantia had restored him to full health. Tom laughed and Storm let out a neigh of pleasure. The four friends were united once more!

Then Silver padded over to Tom and dropped something from his mouth. It lay shining on the ground – an amber jewel!

Tom picked it up. "It's from the mammoth's tusk," he said. "Thank you, Silver."

He slipped the jewel into place on his magic belt. Immediately he felt a new power flowing through him. He turned to Elenna.

"The amber jewel is working!" he told her. "It will help me to be a better fighter – my battle skills already feel so much sharper!"

His body filled with renewed strength, Tom threw his sword high in the air and caught it with a shout. "I pity the next Beast that tries to stop us!" he laughed. "Let's get out of here – I'm sure there will be food and beds at the rebel camp!"

But as they stepped out of the forest, Tom could not shake off memories of the gatekeeper's warning.

What was waiting for him back in Avantia? He'd find out soon enough. But first, there was another evil Beast to defeat.

Join Tom on the next stage
of the Beast Quest

Meet

STinG
THE SCORPION
MAN

Can Tom free the good Beasts from
the Dark Realm?

PROLOGUE

The Gorgonian medicine woman twitched and muttered in her sleep. Her dreams were strange tonight.

A boy stood alone in a dark tunnel, his face bloody and streaked with sweat. In his hand was a battered wooden shield with six tokens embedded in its surface. Torches flickered along the long passageway, throwing the boy's shadow onto the wall, where it stood huge and alone.

The boy was suddenly dwarfed by a second silhouette – a Beast with a sweeping tail and monstrous pincers which snipped and slashed at the air.

A giant scorpion!

The medicine woman moaned in her sleep as the silhouette grew clearer. The creature was more than a scorpion. It was half-man!

The boy whirled around, raising his sword, as the Beast attacked with its razor-sharp pincers.

"Tom!"

A girl's voice screamed. It was Elenna, the

girl the medicine woman had helped to heal. She stood with a wolf by her side and held a bow with an arrow in the bow-string. She let the arrow fly at the scorpion, but it bounced harmlessly off the creature's body. The boy stumbled and the Beast reared up, its pincers snapping viciously and slicing ever closer to the boy's head.

The medicine woman woke from her dream with a gasp. She sat upright, clutching her blankets, her heart hammering. A tiny scorpion lay at the bottom of her bed. She got up, her eyes never leaving the creature's glossy black body. Her nightmare had saved her life. Many Gorgonians had been found dead in their beds because a poisonous scorpion had found its way under the covers.

She pushed her way out of the tent. The boy's face was still clear in her mind. Tom. She had heard that name recently. Elenna had mentioned it. Tom was her friend.

Shivering, the old woman tried to shake off the feeling of dread that had crept over her. The dream was a sign of things to come. She'd had premonitions before. She hoped this one was wrong.

"Stay safe, Elenna and Tom," she muttered, gazing up at the swirling red sky of Gorgonia.

Scorpions were bad enough.

A giant scorpion would be unstoppable.

CHAPTER ONE

DESTINY IN THE WEST

The blood-red light from the Gorgonian sunrise peeped through the trees as Tom and Elenna made their way out of the forest, their faithful companions, Storm and Silver, ambling beside them. Vulture-like birds croaked on the branches overhead, and a thick mist lay on the ground.

Tom led the way, holding Storm's bridle. He noticed that Elenna kept her hand protectively on one of Silver's shaggy shoulders. The wolf had been badly wounded two Quests previously, and had only just returned to Elenna's side. Tom and his friends had already freed five of Avantia's Beasts from Malvel's kingdom. Arcta the mountain giant was the last of the six Beasts being kept here against his will by the evil wizard. If they could free Arcta, their Quest would be complete.

Tom pulled his shield from his shoulder and studied the tokens set into its scarred wooden surface.

Gifts from the good Beasts, they usually glowed and vibrated when a Beast was in danger. But Arcta's eagle feather remained dark, and the shield had been still for far too long. Where was Malvel keeping the mountain giant?

"Still nothing?" Elenna asked.

Tom shook his head. "It's as if Arcta is somewhere so far away that the shield can't sense him." He pushed his shield over his shoulder again, refusing to meet Elenna's eyes. He didn't want to reveal his worst fear: that Arcta was already dead. "Perhaps the map will give us some clues," he said instead.

He took the smelly, worn parchment from Storm's saddlebag. Malvel had given them the map when they first entered Gorgonia. Each time they began searching for a good Beast the map would give Tom a sign that he could use, or a green line would snake across its surface for Tom and Elenna to follow. Usually these signs and pathways would lead to trouble, but it was the only map that Tom and Elenna had.

"Nothing," Tom said, looking down at the

map in disappointment.

"We can't trust it anyway," Elenna pointed out as Tom put the map away.

"You're right," Tom replied. "I'll use my compass instead. It won't let us down."

Tom's uncle had given him the silver compass on his first birthday as a hero. Instead of north, south, east and west, the words Destiny and Danger were inscribed upon its face. The compass had belonged to his father, Taladon, who was once the Master of the Beasts for Avantia and had disappeared when Tom was a baby.

Tom held the compass and walked in a complete circle. As he pointed it to the west, the arrow whirled several times and came to rest on Destiny.

Tom felt his heart lift. He put the compass away. "The compass is telling us to go west," he said to Elenna. "I'm sure that's where Arcta is. While there's blood in my veins, I will find him and get him home to Avantia!"

Storm neighed and tossed his black mane as if he were agreeing. Silver sprang ahead down the path, eager to get going, and Tom and

Elenna pressed on after him.

In the far distance, they saw something lying on the ground.

"What's that?" Elenna asked, shading her eyes in the red light.

Tom used the power of the magical golden helmet to bring the object into focus. Although the precious golden armour had been returned to Avantia at the end of the last Quest, he still possessed its gifts, and the helmet gave him extra-keen vision.

It was a boy, sprawled on the ground and riddled with arrows. His body was twitching. Tom felt his skin turn cold.

"It's Seth," he said to Elenna. "He's hurt."

Seth was one of Malvel's servants. Tom and Elenna had fought him before, and the boy had been intent on killing them.

"Do we help?" Elenna asked.

Tom hesitated.

Seth was his sworn enemy. What should he do?

Follow this Quest to the end in STING THE SCORPION MAN.

Win an exclusive
Beast Quest T-shirt and goody bag!

In every Beast Quest book the Beast Quest logo is hidden
in one of the pictures. Find the logo in this book and
make a note of which page it appears on.
Send the page number in to us.
Each month we will draw one winner to receive
a Beast Quest T-shirt and goody bag.

Send your entry on a postcard listing
the title of this book and the winning
page number to:

THE BEAST QUEST COMPETITION:
TUSK THE MIGHTY MAMMOTH
Orchard Books
338 Euston Road, London NW1 3BH
Australian readers should email:
childrens.books@hachette.com.au

New Zealand readers should write to:
Beast Quest Competition
4 Whetu Place, Mairangi Bay, Auckland, NZ
or email: childrensbooks@hachette.co.nz

Only one entry per child.
Final draw: 31 October 2009

You can also enter this competition
via the Beast Quest website: www.beastquest.co.uk

Beast Quest ®

Fight the Beasts,
Fear the Magic

www.beastquest.co.uk

Have you checked out the all-new Beast Quest website?
It's the place to go for games, downloads, activities,
sneak previews and lots of fun!

You can read all about your favourite Beast Quest
monsters, download free screensavers and desktop
wallpapers for your computer, and send
beastly e-cards to your friends.

Sign up to the newsletter at www.beastquest.co.uk
to receive exclusive extra content and the opportunity
to enter special members-only competitions. It's the best
place to go for up-to-date info on all the Beast Quest
books, including the next exciting series,
which features six brand new Beasts.

Series 1

Ferno the Fire Dragon	978 1 84616 483 5
Sepron the Sea Serpent	978 1 84616 482 8
Arcta the Mountain Giant	978 1 84616 484 ?
Tagus the Horse-Man	978 1 84616 4?
Nanook the Snow Monster	978 1 84616 o
Epos the Flame Bird	978 1 84616 ? 5

Vedra & Krimon: Twin Beasts of Avantia	978 1 84616 951 9

Series 2: The Golden Armour

Zepha the Monster Squid	978 1 84616 988 5
Claw the Giant Monkey	978 1 84616 989 2
Soltra the Stone Charmer	978 1 84616 990 8
Vipero the Snake Man	978 1 84616 991 5
Arachnid the King of Spiders	978 1 84616 992 2
Trillion the Three-Headed Lion	978 1 84616 993 9

Spiros the Ghost Phoenix	978 1 84616 994 6

Series 3: The Dark Realm

Torgor the Minotaur	978 1 84616 997 7
Skor the Winged Stallion	978 1 84616 998 4
Narga the Sea Monster	978 1 40830 000 8
Kaymon the Gorgon Hound	978 1 40830 001 5
Tusk the Mighty Mammoth	978 1 40830 002 2
Sting the Scorpion Man	978 1 40830 003 9

All priced at £4.99

Vedra & Krimon: Twin Beasts of Avantia and *Spiros the Ghost Phoenix* are priced at £5.99

The Beast Quest books are available from all good
bookshops, or can be ordered direct from the publisher:
Orchard Books, PO BOX 29, Douglas IM99 1BQ.
Credit card orders please telephone 01624 836000
or fax 01624 837033 or visit our website: www.orchardbooks.co.uk
or e-mail: bookshop@enterprise.net for details.

To order please quote title, author
and ISBN and your full name and address.
Cheques and postal orders should be made payable to 'Bookpost plc.'
Postage and packing is FREE within the UK
(overseas customers should add £2.00 per book).

Prices and availability are subject to change